I Owe You One

ORCA
YOUNG
READERS

I Owe You One

Natalie Hyde

ORCA BOOK PUBLISHERS

Library and Archives Canada Cataloguing in Publication

Hyde, Natalie, 1963-
I owe you one / Natalie Hyde.
(Orca young readers)

Issued also in electronic format.
ISBN 978-1-55469-414-3

I. Title. II. Series: Orca young readers
PS8615.Y33I17 2011   JC813'.6   C2011-903478-6

First published in the United States, 2011
Library of Congress Control Number: 2011929253

Summary: After an old lady rescues him from drowning, Wes considers how to honor his
dead father's wishes while repaying what his friend Zach calls a life debt.

*Orca Book Publishers is dedicated to preserving the environment and has printed this book
on paper certified by the Forest Stewardship Council®.*

Orca Book Publishers gratefully acknowledges the support for its publishing programs
provided by the following agencies: the Government of Canada through the
Canada Book Fund and the Canada Council for the Arts, and the Province of
British Columbia through the BC Arts Council and the Book Publishing Tax Credit.

Cover artwork by Peter Ferguson
Author photo by Brad Scott

ORCA BOOK PUBLISHERS   ORCA BOOK PUBLISHERS
PO Box 5626, Stn. B   PO Box 468
Victoria, BC Canada   Custer, WA USA
V8R 6S4   98240-0468

www.orcabook.com
Printed and bound in Canada.

14 13 12 11 • 4 3 2 1

For Nathan, who loves a good explosion

Chapter 1

Inch by inch, I leaned farther out over the swollen spring creek. My left hand clutched a slippery tree trunk while my right hand reached for my favorite ballcap. It was dangling at the very tip of a narrow limb hanging over the water, and it looked like the wind would rip it off and send it down the surging creek at any moment.

My mom would kill me if she knew I was this close to the flooding creek, but I was desperate.

I heard footsteps crunching on the gravel path. My heart pounded. I was about to be caught doing the dumbest thing I had ever done. Well, maybe not the dumbest. There was that whole slime-mold experiment last summer. We couldn't use our bathtub for a month.

I made one last grab for my hat.

You know, everything really does warp into slow motion when you are heading for disaster. And I certainly was. The May rains that had turned the normally quiet creek into a raging torrent had also turned the bank into a greasy chute heading straight for the water. As I lunged for my cap, I lost my balance. My feet jerked out from under me and I landed— *splat!*—in the mud and began sliding headfirst down the slippery bank. Just before my face hit the water, my right hand grabbed a root and I whipped around, almost dislocating my shoulder.

And there I lay, half in and half out of the icy spring runoff while the angry current pulled at my legs. I held on to that gnarled root with a mighty grip. My other hand groped in the leaves and mud for a way to haul myself out of there.

"Help!" I yelled into the wind. "Is anyone out there?"

I was saved from certain death by Mrs. Minton (who's got to be at least eighty) and her old wooden cane. She was hanging on to a tree with all her strength. I could see her mouth opening and closing, but between the rushing of the water and the pounding of the blood in my ears, I couldn't hear what she was saying.

I consider myself pretty strong for an eleven-year-old, but it took every ounce of energy I had to put one hand over the other on that cane and pull myself out of the creek. It didn't help that the cane was covered with little metal souvenir crests from Mrs. Minton's trips to Europe. Every time my hand moved up the cane, the crests cut into my flesh.

Standing on the muddy bank, shaking with the cold, my hands bleeding, I didn't know which was worse: the trouble I would be in from my mom, or the teasing I was going to get from Zach for being rescued by an old lady and her cane. It was a tough call.

"Wesley James Morgan," she said, "are you trying to get yourself killed?"

Old people and your parents are the only ones allowed to get away with calling you by your whole name. I hate the name Wesley. No one—I mean no one—calls me Wesley. It's Wes. Always Wes.

"N-n-no," I said, my teeth chattering uncontrollably. "I was t-t-trying t-to get m-m-my hat b-b-back."

"You kids!" she said, smiling and wrapping me in her heavy crocheted shawl. "Never seeing danger.

I was just like that." It was a real granny shawl, multicolored, with purple and pink fringe. If any of my friends had walked by right then and seen me in that shawl, I probably would have jumped back in the creek.

I watched in disbelief as she used the tip of her cane to snag my hat and present it to me with a shake of her head. "I bet your mother would be none too happy to hear her only son was almost washed away for the sake of a baseball cap."

The chattering was worse now that the wind was turning my soaking wet clothes to ice, so I didn't try to reply. No use explaining to her that my dad had bought me the hat on our last vacation together.

"Well, it was providential that I decided to go for a walk today, despite what the wind does to my hair."

"Are you g-g-going to t-t-tell my m-m-mom what happ-p-pened?"

Mrs. Minton thought for a moment. "I guess if the Fates had wanted you to get into trouble with your mother, they would have sent her to walk your dog instead of giving me the idea of getting some fresh air. Come along, Wesley. You can dry off at my house."

So that's how I came to be sitting in Mrs. Minton's living room, covered in two afghans, my feet stuffed into huge furry moose slippers, sipping steaming hot chocolate while she threw most of my clothes in her dryer. Some things I left on even though they were wet.

I had never been in Mrs. Minton's house before, and it was nothing like I expected. No flowered couches, cats or cabinets full of teacups. Instead, every available inch of space—the walls, the fireplace mantel, all the tables—was covered with photographs. These weren't your average family pictures of smiling babies and graduations though. In one picture a group of women in yellow crash helmets stood on a rocky shore, holding up their paddles in front of enormous rapids. Other photos showed a parachutist's feet hitting the ground, a young woman hugging a koala, smiling men in red parkas on a snowy mountain. There was an old brownish photo of a downhill skier with no helmet. She was caught mid-flight, bright-eyed, her curly hair streaming out behind her. Mrs. Minton's house was full of people having adventures.

I tried to picture Mrs. Minton having an adventure. I couldn't.

"Are these people your family?" I asked.

Mrs. Minton smiled. "They are." She set a plate of shortbread down in front of me and pointed to the pictures. "This is my nephew Bill parachuting in France. And that's my granddaughter Rachel with the koala in Australia. She's on the national ski team now, you know. She has her first big race as a team member this July in Chile."

"In the summer?"

"It will be winter in the southern hemisphere, Wesley."

"Oh." My eyes shot back to the picture of the skier with the curly hair. Mrs. Minton followed my eyes.

"You'd never guess that only thirteen seconds after this picture was taken, I would take a spill and blow out my knee, would you?"

"That's *you*?" I tried really hard to believe that the daring, wild woman in the picture was old Mrs. Minton.

She laughed. "I wasn't born this old, you know. And once I get my hip replacement, I might just strap on a pair of skis for old times' sake."

I couldn't tell if she was joking or not.

"Did you win any races?" I asked.

"I had my moments, but I was never as good as Rachel. Her mother had her skiing before she could walk." Mrs. Minton laughed a little as she passed me a picture of a tiny girl on two stubby skis. She was stuffed into a snowsuit so puffy that she looked like a pink marshmallow with legs. I smiled as I handed the picture back and pointed to another one on the mantel.

"Who are those men on the mountain?" I asked.

"That's my father and three of his friends at Base Camp One on Mount Everest."

Mount Everest! I would have jumped up to take a closer look, but I was pinned down by the afghans. Why couldn't I have been rescued by a mountaineer with cool equipment?

"I think I'd better get going before my mom wonders what happened to me," I said.

Mrs. Minton nodded. "Let me grab your things. They should be pretty dry now."

She came back with my clothes, and I shuffled to the bathroom to change.

Dressed again, I hurried to the front door.

"Um, thanks," I said, looking at the floor, one hand on the doorknob. "For saving my life and all that."

She paused before asking, "What made you risk your life for a ballcap anyway? Don't you kids have dozens of those things?"

"My dad gave it to me," I said, trying to keep my voice steady.

There was a long silence as my words hung in the air. "I was really sorry to hear about his passing, Wesley," she finally said. "Such a good man."

I didn't trust myself to speak, so I just nodded.

"Well, just promise me you'll stay away from that creek until it settles down. There's no telling when I'll feel up to another walk."

I looked up just in time to see Mrs. Minton smile. I try not to look at old people when thcy smile. There's nothing worse than seeing their false teeth slip, so I was relieved to see that Mrs. Minton seemed to still have all her original teeth. And it wasn't just a little grin. It made her whole face light up, and it made me smile too.

I thanked her again and slipped out the front door, terrified that someone would see me. I jogged down her front path, trying to get out of the danger zone. I almost made it. I was just closing her gate when my best friend Zach came around the corner.

"Hey, Wes!" he called. "Where've you been? I've been looking for you for half an hour." He looked down at my hand, which was still on the gate, and back up at my face.

"Uh, I was just…" For a split second I considered telling him a new and improved version of my adventure. In it I was the hero who risked his life to save old Mrs. Minton, whose cane got tangled in the bushes. Weak and confused, she was about to slip down the muddy bank to a certain death. While valiantly holding on to her, a freak gust of wind blew me into the roaring creek and I was nearly swept away. Coming up for one last gasp of air, my life flashed before my eyes, and I managed to grab a branch, haul myself out and drag her away from the bank to safety too.

Unfortunately I am a terrible liar. My dad used to say I should never play poker because my face was so easy to read. He always knew right away who had taken the last slice of pizza from the fridge or that I had been given a blue slip for not having my homework done.

And Zach was the last person I could fool. We'd been friends since we were old enough to throw sand in each other's faces in the sandbox. I was going to have to tell him everything.

I got off easy. Zach only laughed once. The thought of me under Mrs. Minton's afghans wearing only my underwear and some fuzzy moose slippers was too much for him.

Chapter 2

Two weeks later, I was pretty sure that Zach had forgotten the whole rescue thing with Mrs. Minton. I could turn my attention to more important matters.

"How steep do you think it is?" I asked Zach as I rode my bicycle through the old gate that he held open for me.

"It's like a wall! Straight up!"

"Remind me again why we're going across—umpfh—Mr. Delany's empty field—ouch—on our bikes?"

"You want—ow—to try it out, don't you?"

At the rate we were going, our bikes would be wrecked before we got to the hill. But Zach was right. I did want to try it out. The land around Six Roads, the little town where we lived, was basically limestone cliffs and trees. Not exactly the ideal place for dirt biking. To locate a hill that wasn't just a pile of rocks was a major find. The perfect thing for when I finally got my 250cc Hummer dirt bike.

"How'd you find it?" I asked.

"Some professor is interested in the old Indian copper mine my dad found when he—*ouch*—was doing survey work. He asked Dad to show him the location, and I went with them. While they were—*umpfh*—crawling around looking for the entrance, I climbed up the cliff and had a look around. This hill has been hiding in the corner of Delany's land all the time!"

"Are we—*ow*—almost there?"

Zach stopped his bike to let me catch up. I was glad he did. My teeth were aching from going over all the ruts, and I was sweating. I was glad I hadn't worn my jacket.

"It's just over there," he said, pointing to a stand of trees that was fenced off from the huge field.

It took a few more minutes of tooth-rattling riding to get there.

"We just need to take down a couple of these rails so we can get our bikes in," Zach said. "There's a sort of path through the trees."

I looked around, feeling a little nervous. It was an unwritten rule in the country that you never damaged fences.

"There aren't any animals in this field, are there?" It was a huge pasture, and I couldn't see the far end of it around the trees.

Zach shook his head. "I didn't see anything in here the other day when I checked it out. Besides, the Delanys don't have cattle."

"Are you sure they won't mind us riding on their property?"

Zach sighed. "Why are you such a wimp today?"

I didn't want to tell him that one close call on my life per month was my limit. And I didn't need to get into any trouble with my mom. I was pretty sure she had figured out what had happened at the creek a couple of weeks ago. She had looked suspiciously at my clothes and sniffed them with this funny look on her face.

"Okay, but this better be good." Together we wrestled the rails off and laid them on the ground.

We pushed our bikes through, and Zach hopped on his.

"Shouldn't we replace these rails?" I asked.

"Nah. Then we'd just have to do it all over again when we leave."

I listened for a moment. There was no movement. No sound of a stampede. Zach was right. The field was empty.

The path wound between a few scraggly pine trees. Within a few seconds, it became obvious why the woodlot was fenced off. The land dipped down into a gully that was swampland. I skidded to a stop.

"How are we supposed to get through that?"

Zach pointed to a couple of boards straddling some stones poking out of the swamp. They made a rickety sort of boardwalk through the narrowest part, and he stood on the pedals as he bounced across.

I was going to tell Zach to forget it, but then I saw it. On the other side of the swamp, the land leveled and then swooped up into an impressive tower of dirt. The sides were steep and the top was flat. It looked just like the hills in motocross races I had watched on TV.

I rolled down to the swamp and inched my way across the boards to where Zach was waiting.

14

Bushes and rocks made it hard to get up any speed before attacking the hill, but we managed to get about halfway up before getting off and pushing our bikes up the rest of the way. It would be better on my Hummer. I could just rev up the engine and conquer the hill.

"You were right, Zach. This hill is awesome," I said as we rested at the top.

"I told you. And just think—" Zach stopped talking as we both heard a sound. A sound that didn't belong in an empty field.

We looked at each other in horror.

"You didn't just hear a neigh, did you?" I asked, hoping I had imagined it.

"Uh, maybe?"

The blood drained from my face as I turned my bike and headed back down the hill. If I had dared to take a hand off my handlebars, I would have smacked myself on the forehead. How could I have forgotten that the Delanys kept horses? They were so proud of their trotters or pacers or whatever they called them.

We had to get back to the fence and fix it. Fast. Before the horses got in.

I was almost back to the boardwalk across the swamp when my heart sank. We were too late.

One of the horses was not only inside the fenced-off area, it was in the swamp. It was struggling to pull its legs out of the mud, and the whites of its eyes were showing as it tossed its head and neighed.

Zach panicked. Maybe because he realized this was *all his fault*. "What is it doing in there?!" he screeched.

"Well, it's not line dancing," I yelled back, my panic turning to anger as I realized I was going to be in it as deep as the horse if my mother or the Delanys found out.

Our screams scared the horse, and it struggled even more and sank even deeper into the mud.

A couple more horses were at the top of the rise, ready to head for the swamp.

"Zach, chase those other horses back into the field while I try to help this one."

Zach dropped his bike and ran toward the horses, waving his arms. They scattered at the sight of him and turned back along the path to the dismantled fence. Then one skittered sideways and started down the incline toward the swamp.

"Get him! GET HIM!" I yelled, terrified we would soon have two horses stuck in the mud.

"I'm trying!"

"Take off your shirt."

"What?"

"Take off your shirt and wave it like flag."

The horse in the mud neighed again, and the loose one responded. They were probably telling each other what a bad idea it had been to go through that hole in the fence. It was exactly what Zach and I were thinking.

Zach whipped off his yellow T-shirt and held it out in front of him like a matador's cape.

I tried to get close to the stuck horse by stepping on some rocks. If I could grab its halter, maybe I could direct it out of the deep mud.

Zach inched toward the loose horse slowly, gently shaking the shirt. The horse eyed it suspiciously and took another step toward his pal in the swamp. Zach backed up to try and come between them.

I put one foot on a clump of grass. Neither Zach nor I made a sound in case we spooked the horses again. My fingers barely touched the halter. A couple more inches and I could get a hold of it.

Zach stepped back and to his left.

I stretched out as far as I could and curled my finger around the metal loop on the halter. I had him.

At the sudden pressure on his halter, the horse in the mud flung its head back, taking me with it. And there I hung, yelling, my legs kicking frantically, trying to find the ground again.

The other horse startled and lunged forward. Zach scrambled backward, lost his footing and toppled into the thick layer of muck.

"What in the blazes is going on?!"

The voice belonged to Mrs. Delany, and, man, did she sound furious.

Zach and I froze. He was sitting, shirtless, in the mud, and I was hanging in midair from the halter. I felt my cold fingers begin to slip, and I seemed to hover in the air for a second before I landed facedown in cold, slimy mud. It oozed between my fingers as I pushed myself back up.

"Of all the ignorant, irresponsible, clueless acts of vandalism I have ever seen…," Mrs. Delany yelled. I was sure she had this lecture memorized. When her five sons were little, they were the terrors of Six Roads. She would have continued, I'm sure, but just then Mr. Delany appeared at the top of the rise.

"Get the tractor, Bill," Mrs. Delany said. "Domino here is right stuck."

She ignored us as she unclipped a lead line hanging from her jeans and walked slowly up to the loose horse, clipped the line to his halter and tied him to a nearby pine. Then she spoke softly to the horse in the mud until it calmed down and stopped struggling.

Zach and I pulled ourselves out of the mud and stood off to the side, shivering. I felt just about as stupid as I could be.

Mr. Delany came back on the tractor, and he and Mrs. Delany both ignored us as they attached a wide leather strap to one of the chains on the back of the tractor. It looked kind of like what tow trucks use. Mrs. Delany stood on the boards and slipped the strap under the horse's belly just behind its front legs and snapped the other end to another chain. Mr. Delany edged the tractor forward while Mrs. Delany pulled on the horse's halter and encouraged the horse to try and move.

It worked. He heaved and bucked out of the muck, then stood at the edge of the swamp while Mrs. Delany ran her hands down his muddy legs.

"Looks like he didn't pull or break anything."

I let out the breath I didn't realize I was holding. The rest of the lecture was sure to come now. And our punishment.

"You should both know better." She shook her head as she looked at us. What would it be? Mucking out the stables for a month? Checking and repairing all the fences around their sixty-acre property?

Nope. It was none of those things. In fact she didn't mention any punishment at all. The grossest chore in the world would have been easier to take than the words she said. "Wes, if your father could see you now, he would be sorely disappointed in you."

Chapter 3

From behind, I'm sure we looked like two bowlegged cowboys as we walked our bikes back out of the field, trying not to let our clammy, stinky jeans touch us more than necessary. We had apologized over and over to the Delanys before we left, but they just glared at us.

"Man, I'm going to be grounded for the entire summer for this one," I said.

"We can go to my house first and use the hose to wash the mud off," Zach said. "Then we just have to find some place to hide out until our clothes dry."

"That'll never work. My mom has this spidey sense when something bad happens. It's like she can smell trouble. It's spooky. And this mud's not going to come off with a hose. As soon as the Delanys call my mom, I'll be grounded for the rest of the school year. Probably the whole summer too."

"I don't think the Delanys will call."

"Why not?"

"'Cause they're probably leaving for that big race weekend out in Humber tonight. They'll be too busy getting ready."

"I don't know," I said slowly. I wanted to believe that we could be that lucky, but it seemed too good to be true.

"And it's not like they're gonna get all superior after some of the stuff their kids pulled. Wasn't your dad one of the ones who helped pull their car out when Brian Delany rolled it into Waseeka Lake?"

"Yeah, but…"

"All we gotta do is get clean, and our moms won't suspect a thing."

"Well," I said, hoping beyond hope that Zach was right, "there is one person who might help us."

"Who?"

I don't know why I thought of Mrs. Minton. Maybe because she seemed so understanding the last time I was in a mess.

We took the back way to Mrs. Minton's so as not to have to go past my house.

We were just about there when we heard a loud bang. I almost lost my grip on my bike as the ground shook.

We looked at each other.

"Daryl," we both said at the same time.

"I don't know why he didn't just join the army when he turned eighteen. Then he could have spent the last five years blowing things up as a job instead of doing it as a hobby," I said.

"Maybe he thinks groundhogs are the enemy? You know, sneaking around in underground tunnels."

"I think he just likes blowing things up," I said. There was a rumor around town that Daryl was a few bricks short of a load. But Mom said every small town had its oddball, and I guessed Daryl was ours. Besides, he never hurt anyone. Even the groundhogs seemed pretty safe. They'd pop their heads up, and by the time he set the charges and hit the button, they'd be miles away watching from another hole. I swore they thought it was a sport and even enjoyed it.

We rounded the corner onto Fraserwood Street, left our bikes by the gate and walked up to Mrs. Minton's door.

I was trying to think up a good explanation for how my clothes got all muddy again when she opened the door. Her bright blue eyes looked us up and down.

"You two smell like a stagnant pond. What was it this time, Wesley? Mud boarding? Dumpster diving? Swamp surfing?"

For a second my mind wandered, thinking how cool mud boarding sounded. Then I pictured my mom finding me like this and I came back to earth.

"One of the Delanys' horses got stuck in a swamp and we helped get it out," Zach said.

Mrs. Minton raised an eyebrow. "You want to tell me what *really* happened, Wesley?"

There was no point lying. Like I said, I'm a terrible liar. I told her about everything—the supposedly empty field, the rail fence, the motocross hill and the rescue of the stuck horse.

She didn't say anything for a moment, but the corners of her mouth were twitching as she said, "And I suppose you've come here hoping I'll have mercy on you and help clean you up to escape your parents' wrath?"

"We didn't mean to do anything wrong," I said.

"And we were doing our best to get the horses out of there," Zach said.

"And we offered to fix their fence," I added.

"And if we had seen or heard any animals in the field, we never would have—"

Zach was cut off by Mrs. Minton holding up her hands in surrender. "All right, boys. You're lucky my washing machine is only half full. I was waiting until after I finished changing the oil on my Mustang to wash my dirty clothes."

"Thanks, Mrs. Minton," I said.

Mrs. Minton shook her head as she let us in. "You are so like you father, Wesley."

"My father?"

"He sure was one for getting into scrapes when he was little."

I couldn't believe it. Mr. "Highest Respect in the County" got into scrapes?

"But he was the most decorated fire chief in the region's history," Zach said.

Mrs. Minton nodded. "He grew into a man of courage and integrity." She smiled at me as she handed me an afghan and the moose slippers. "Which is why I still hold out hope for you, Wesley." She laughed a little as I waddled into the bathroom to get out of my muddy clothes.

I couldn't even imagine that I'd ever be as brave, calm and strong as my dad. "I wouldn't even know where to begin," I mumbled.

Mrs. Minton smiled a broad, warm smile. "Yes, you would."

Chapter 4

My only consolation that day was that Zach could never again make fun of me for the afghan/moose-slipper thing. Not when he was wrapped in a quilt that had bonneted dolls in every square and his feet were covered in hand-knit lime green socks. I almost choked on my cookie when I saw him waddle out of the bathroom.

"What are these, anyway?" I asked Mrs. Minton, biting into the hard, crunchy cookie.

"Biscotti. They're Italian and very good for dunking." She took hers and plunked it into her mug.

Zach and I dunked ours into our hot chocolate. She was right. The hot liquid made them soft and delicious.

"So," I said, almost afraid to ask, "are you going to tell our moms?"

Mrs. Minton looked thoughtful. "Well, I can't get one of you into trouble without getting the other one in it too. And I'm not too fond of the idea of bothering your mother with this, Wesley." She put her coffee down and looked across the room at a picture of a young man in army uniform. I was pretty sure it was Mr. Minton.

"The first couple of years after a woman loses her husband are very hard. Your mother certainly doesn't need any extra worries right now." She looked back at me. "But honestly, Wesley, you need to tone it down a bit. My hip surgery has been moved up to the week after next, so I'll be out of commission for a while. I won't be able to rescue you for at least a couple of months."

I nodded, but Mrs. Minton's face clouded over.

"It'll be good to have the surgery over with, won't it?" Zach asked, seeing her face.

"Oh yes, but I was planning on going to Chile to watch Rachel's race. I had my ticket and everything. The surgery was originally scheduled for after I got back." She sighed. "I had to cancel all my plans, but the doctor said I was lucky to get in early. Still, I hate

28

to disappoint Rachel. Now I'll have to just watch it on TV, I guess." She looked over at the small set. "I just hope the picture will come in clearly. Maybe I need new rabbit ears?"

"Why don't you get a satellite dish, Mrs. M.? We get two hundred channels!" Zach said.

"Do you know what a fixed income is, Zachariah?" she asked.

Zach shook his head.

"It means that even if I could figure out those remote control things, I couldn't afford satellite. Besides, rabbit ears aren't so bad. I get most of the programs I like to watch on the six channels I pick up with them. I can even get channel fifty-six if the wind is blowing in the right direction."

We left Mrs. Minton's feeling guilty but smelling mountain-fresh.

I spent the rest of the night at home jumping out of my skin every time the phone rang, sure that the Delanys would call. But my mother never came into my room with that look on her face—the look that said my summer would be better spent helping around the house than having fun. The look that said I needed to build my character and learn some responsibility.

your own death." He paused for dramatic effect. I was starting to sweat again. All I could hear were my dad's words in my head. *A man always pays his debts, Wes*.

Most guys only have to hear that kind of fatherly advice once in a while. Usually when they get in trouble. When my dad knew he wasn't going to be around all that long, he started throwing around advice at every possible opportunity. It was like an avalanche of wisdom on everything from why I shouldn't throw spitballs at girls (*A man always treats a woman with respect, Wes. You'll understand why that's important someday*) to why I had to turn in the lottery ticket I found outside Lee's (*A man doesn't keep what doesn't belong to him, Wes*).

"In other cultures," Zach said, "you'd be her slave, forced to do chores like cleaning her dentures and vacuuming." He looked like he was enjoying this.

"She doesn't have false teeth," I said. I knew he was going to ask me how I knew that, but we had arrived at Lee's, and I quickly opened the door and went inside. With any luck, Zach would forget all about my debt to Mrs. Minton.

Mrs. Lee was at her usual post behind the counter. "Hi, boys! We got new magazines in."

Mrs. Lee ran the store like a garage sale. Everything was jumbled up and stuffed in wherever it fit. She didn't believe in throwing anything away either. The bells that rang when you ran over the cable at the gas pumps came off the old *Nice 'n Icy* ice-cream truck parked out back. The rags Mr. Lee used to wipe off his squeegee looked like cut-up flannel nighties.

I passed the empty chocolate-bar boxes filled with fishing lures, and the postcard rack stuffed with packages of spices and rolled-up Chinese calendars, and went straight for the magazines, hoping the new *Wizard* was in. *Wizard* is all about comic books. At the back, it lists how much you can get for some really old ones. It was there on the rack, and I opened it to the price lists.

"Holy crow, Zach! My comic is up to eight hundred dollars already!"

"You gonna sell?"

"Nah. I want to wait till it's worth enough to buy a dirt bike."

He looked over at me, his forehead crinkled. "But eight hundred dollars can get you a bike right now, and Frank would snap up your comic in a second. I think that's the only issue he doesn't have."

"I know, I know. Every time I go near him, he asks me. But it's still not enough for a two-fifty-cc Hummer. Even used, they're about twice that."

Zach just shrugged. He wouldn't know a 250cc Hummer if he tripped over one. One dirt bike was just like the next to him. But ask him about fiberglass versus wooden hockey sticks, and he would go on for about an hour. He was a hockey nut, even though he hadn't played since he was little.

I wasn't going to settle for just any dirt bike though. My dad and I had spent hours going over all the brochures. We had worked out what permits I'd need and where I would ride. He was going to supervise because I was still underage. That wasn't going to happen now. By the time I got my bike though, I'd probably be old enough to ride wherever I wanted. If I closed my eyes, I could almost feel myself racing across the fields with the hum of the engine in my ears.

I grabbed some nacho chips. As I headed for the cash, the ground shook. Without lifting her eyes from the newspaper she was reading, Mrs. Lee reached out to the shelf behind her to keep the jars of olives from falling.

"Daryl," she said shaking her head.

Everyone in Six Roads was used to Daryl and his explosions. People didn't rush outside anymore thinking it was an earthquake.

Another blast shook the ground. This time it seemed a lot bigger. Then we heard a huge bang, and the ground shook again.

"That sounds no good." Mrs. Lee looked worried. "I hope Daryl is okay."

You wouldn't think Mrs. Lee would have a soft spot for someone like Daryl, especially after all the jars of pickles and salsa that had fallen and broken because of the blasts, but she did. She said he reminded her of her brother in China.

"We'll check it out, Mrs. Lee," I said as Zach and I took off out of the store.

"You make sure Daryl okay, okay?" she called after us as we hopped on our bikes.

Daryl's place wasn't too far out of town, but when we finally got there, the house was deserted.

"I think the blast came from back that way," I said, pointing to the hayfield at the far end of Daryl's property.

We raced down the tractor path to the back forty. When we reached the field, we spotted him. He was at the base of the hill just past his property line. Mrs. Lee was right. What we saw was definitely no good.

Chapter 5

We stood and stared at what used to be the town's television tower. All that was left was a heap of metal and a mangled transmitter.

"See, this is why we got satellite TV," Zach said. "We're too far in the boonies to rely on one television tower."

I groaned. "Well, we still have those stupid rabbit ears. And now I won't be able to watch anything!"

"You can come over to my house."

"This is going to be a lousy summer."

We trooped over to where Daryl was staring at the heap of mangled electronics on the ground.

"Must've set the charge too close to the base," Daryl muttered to himself. "Darn rodents have turned this hill into Swiss cheese."

As if to prove his point, we suddenly felt the ground under our feet shake. But it wasn't another explosion. It was Mr. Elliot barreling across the field from his farm next door, looking mad enough to spit nails.

"What in the name of all that is holy do you think you're doing, Daryl?" Mr. Elliot yelled. Mr. Elliot hated Daryl. Well, maybe *hate* was too strong a word. He called Daryl a loose cannon, which was a pretty good description, seeing as how a few months ago Daryl had almost blown up Mr. Elliot's best cow, Esmeralda. She had wandered a little too close to the fence that separated their farms. I guess Daryl hadn't noticed that the ground-hogs' tunnels ran under both fields. When Daryl blew up the tunnel, the force of the blast had sent Esmeralda flying ten feet in the air. Luckily she'd landed in a clump of junipers and was unhurt, but Mr. Elliot had been furious.

Zach and I had gotten there just as Mr. Elliot saw his best cow staggering to her feet.

"You idiot," he had screamed at Daryl. "Don't you know a cow's like a keg of methane just waiting to go off?"

Daryl had looked at Mr. Elliot in confusion. "Methane?" he asked.

Mr. Elliot walked up to Daryl, put his hands together in front of him and yelled "BOOM!" as his hands flew upward, fingers spread. Finally understanding, Daryl had tried to look serious, but there was this little gleam in his eyes. Really, a flying cow is cool, but an exploding cow! Now there's something you don't see every day.

Since that day, Mr. Elliot has been on full alert where Daryl is concerned. The fact that the cow-blast had unearthed a real Indian arrowhead didn't make any difference to Mr. Elliott. Daryl told him it was a good omen, but Mr. Elliot said he didn't believe in omens.

Everyone else believed it though. What else would explain the fact that only two weeks later, Mr. Elliot got an inheritance from some long-lost uncle? Mr. Elliot insisted it was all just a coincidence, but I heard he kept that arrowhead locked away somewhere safe, just in case.

After the Esmeralda incident, Daryl had kept to himself and stayed away from Mr. Elliot's property. He was on his best behavior. Until today that is.

"I shoulda known you'd be behind this," Mr. Elliot shouted. "You're a menace, that's what you are."

"Maybe it's not as bad as it looks," I said, hoping to calm things down. I went over to the box that protected the transmitter, pulling up a piece of twisted metal to look inside.

What used to be a transmitter was now a jumble of wires, knobs and circuits. Mr. Elliot joined me.

He turned to Daryl, who was standing by, trying to look innocent.

"I…You…This…" was all Mr. Elliot managed. He threw his hands up in the air and walked away.

Chapter 6

We headed home after we told Mrs. Lee that Daryl was okay but the TV tower wasn't.

"How long do you think it will take to get the tower fixed?" I asked.

"Six Roads isn't really on the top of anyone's 'fix it' list," Zach said. "Especially since you and Mrs. Minton are the only people in town without satellite dishes. That tower could be out of commission for weeks— maybe even months."

It wasn't fair. Now that summer vacation was about to start, I would have time to watch TV but I wouldn't have any TV to watch.

I know it was dumb, but I tried the TV almost every day for two weeks, hoping someone had come along and fixed the tower. All I ever got was a screen full of snow. Why couldn't we have gotten satellite too? There were only so many hours I could spend at Zach's house before his mother would start charging me room and board. And I had already beaten every level of *Quinlan's Quest*, *The Firewalker's Fury* and even *Star Lynx* on my Game Box system. It was going to be a long summer.

On Saturday morning I should have been out of the house right after breakfast to catch *Mythbashers* at Zach's house, but it was pouring rain and I was right in the middle of replaying *Quinlan's Quest*, trying to beat my own high score. I was a sitting duck.

"Wesley, can you do me a favor?" my mom called from the kitchen.

Six of the worst words a guy could hear. The favor was always either gross, hard work or embarrassing. Or all three.

"Today, Wesley," she said, louder this time.

I rolled my eyes.

"Stop rolling your eyes and get in here."

How did she do that? Could she hear my eyes rolling?

The smell of banana bread in the kitchen made my mouth water. Mom was in the pantry rummaging around for something. I had the knife in my hand, ready to slice, when she came back in.

"Weapons down," she said, smiling. "You can have some after you take a loaf over to poor Mrs. Minton. I know it's one of her favorites. She's been having a hard time since her hip surgery."

"Why? What happened?" I tried not to look too interested, in case my mom got suspicious as to why I was suddenly concerned about Mrs. Minton.

"She's developed pneumonia and is bedridden. She's got a nurse coming over every day, but I'm hoping some banana bread might cheer her up."

That didn't sound good. I didn't want to go over and see her like that. Not to mention the fact that I had no idea how I was going to pay back my life debt. I knew I was going to feel guilty the minute I looked at her.

She wrapped a loaf and put it in a bag for me. I was going to protest, but she was doing that thing with her eyes. It's like she can see right into my mind. Had she guessed what had happened?

I lowered my eyes, grabbed the bag and let the back screen door slam on the way out. Mom hates that. I peered around the corner of our house before I walked down the driveway. All I could hope was that the rain was keeping everyone inside. Or that my rain hood covered my face. When I saw the coast was clear, I sprinted the two blocks over to Mrs. Minton's house.

I heard Mrs. Minton call for me to come in after I rang the bell. The door was locked, but I knew where the key was hidden. Actually, everyone in Six Roads knew where everyone else's keys were hidden.

Her living room was all changed around since I had been there with Zach after our mud bath. A hospital bed was set up where the couch had been. Beside it was a table with a bunch of medication and cups with straws on it. I didn't realize she was this sick.

"Oh, Wesley! I'm so glad you're here," she said as soon as I took off my shoes. "My TV isn't working properly. Maybe the rabbit ears need turning?"

If only.

"Sorry, Mrs. Minton, but Daryl blew up the TV tower."

"He blew it up? Was it some kind of protest?"

"No, he didn't mean to. He was just fooling around. But the groundhog tunnels ran under the hill, and the whole thing kind of collapsed."

"He probably used too much explosive and the wrong kind of fuse," she sighed.

I looked over at her, wondering what she knew about explosives, and if I should be worried.

"Well, how soon can the tower be fixed?" There was a hint of urgency in her voice.

"Don't know, Mrs. M. We have to find out who to call first. Could be awhile."

"No, no, no," she said, rubbing her crooked hands in agitation.

"Do you want me to get you a couple of movies from Lee's?" I asked. I could understand how bored she must be.

"I don't need a cathode-ray babysitter, Wesley," she snapped.

My eyebrows shot up, partly because I had never heard her angry before and partly because I didn't know what a cathode ray was.

She sighed. "I'm so sorry, Wesley. This isn't your fault. It's just that Rachel's first World Championship race is coming up soon. I promised her I would watch it on TV. She was so disappointed when my hip surgery meant I couldn't be there in person. She said I should watch for a special message from her. If I didn't have pneumonia and this darn hip, I'd go down the road to my friend Margery's house to watch the race, but my doctors say I won't be going anywhere for at least three weeks."

Her eyes glistened, and she twisted her hands together. It didn't seem that big a deal to me to watch some ski race, but maybe when you're eighty-one and not feeling well…maybe she was worried that it was the last race she would ever see.

"Maybe Frank could fix it," I said.

She looked up, her face full of hope. "Yes, yes! Ask Frank. If anyone can fix it, Frank can."

I know I shouldn't have gotten her hopes up, but she looked so sad, and she seemed so much older than the day she had pulled me out of the creek. The surgery and the pneumonia had taken a lot out of her. Her cheeks were hollow, her hands trembled slightly and her eyes had lost their sparkle.

I left, promising to get Frank onto fixing the tower right away, even though secretly I didn't think it would work. It had to be complicated and expensive.

Frank's shop was in a small building beside Lee's. It was floor-to-ceiling appliances and parts for appliances. Lawnmowers, kettles, radios, washing machines. You name it, Frank fixes it. I always thought he could have been an engineer or something, he was that smart. But Frank had dropped out of high school at seventeen to start making money to help feed his five brothers and sisters after their dad got sick.

Problem was, Frank was a bit of a hermit. He almost never left his shop except to go home to his little apartment, and I don't think he even owned a TV. Maybe he was sick of working on them for the past eight years. Anyway, there was no way he would want to trek up to Daryl's farm and face that mess.

It would be easy enough to ask him quickly and then tell Mrs. Minton he couldn't do it. She would be disappointed, I guess, but I'd have kept my promise and then I'd be off the hook.

A man pays his debts, Wes.

The words echoed in my head as I walked. I could picture my dad standing in the hallway in his uniform, ready to face any danger the day might throw at him. I knew what my dad would have done. He never took the easy way out of anything.

Even though I didn't like it, I knew what I had to do. I had to repay my life debt to Mrs. Minton, and fixing the TV tower was how I would do it. It wasn't exactly a life for a life, but it sure seemed important to her. One way or another, I had to make sure that tower got fixed.

I took a detour to Zach's house. I was going to need some backup.

"Well, what do you think?" I asked Zach after I told him my idea.

"I guess it could be considered a life-debt payment," he said. "Especially if it is her final wish."

"I wouldn't call it that. I think she's getting better."

"You don't know for sure. Having her grand-daughter's race to look forward to might give her something to live for. In this documentary I watched the other week, they said a positive attitude helps fight off infection. This could save her life!"

Oh, definitely *National Geographic* talking here.

"But do you think he can fix it?" he asked.

"Frank? Haven't you ever heard the rumors?"

"You mean that Frank can fix anything? I thought that was just a legend."

I shook my head. "I've never seen him beat yet. The trick is going to be convincing him to leave his shop."

"I know. When's the last time you saw him anywhere but in his shop or riding his bike home?"

"Not in recorded history."

"So we're going to have to come up with a way to convince him."

"Leave it to me," I said.

"So, are you ready to sell?" Frank asked me the moment we stepped into his shop.

Frank always greeted me that way. He knew darn well I wasn't going to let go of my Spider-Man comic. "No. I told you. It's an investment," I said.

Frank's face fell. "So, what do you want?"

I launched into the story about Daryl and the TV tower and Mrs. Minton. He wasn't impressed.

I decided to try flattering him. "We need an expert to look at it. Someone who knows what all that junk is."

No response.

"You're so good with electronics and stuff," Zach added.

Nothing.

"Look," I broke in, "Mrs. Minton mentioned you by name. She said if anyone could fix it, you could. She's counting on you."

Frank's face reddened. Bingo. A guilt trip always worked. Frank couldn't disappoint old Mrs. Minton. I remembered that after his dad died, she used to go over and babysit so Frank and his mom could go to work.

With a big sigh, Frank put down the modem he was working on and followed us on his bike to Daryl's farm. After working so hard to get Frank over there, I wasn't too encouraged by the look on his face when he saw the remains of the tower. Zach and I waited, holding our breath.

"Nah," was all he said.

I waited for more, but Frank was apparently finished talking.

"Nah, what?" I asked.

"No use. It's scrap. Can't be fixed."

I stiffened. No way I was going back to Mrs. Minton with that answer.

"What about the legend? That you can fix anything?" I asked. I picked up several of the biggest pieces and held them out to Frank, hoping he'd say he was wrong. He just shook his head.

I let the pieces drop.

Frank turned to go.

"Wait," I said. "What about if we get a new transmitter? Could you install it?"

Never one to waste words, all he said was, "Tower's broken too."

I gritted my teeth.

"We'd get the tower rebuilt, of course," Zach said.

Frank looked uncertain.

"Take some doing," he said.

"But it's possible, right?" I asked.

"Anything's possible…with the right parts," was his answer.

Chapter 7

Zach and I crowded around Frank's desk two days later, trying to hear the person on the other end of his phone. He gave us a dirty look, so we backed off.

He had surfed the Internet for about two hours trying to find a new transmitter. Then he'd spent another twenty minutes phoning around. I was trying hard not to be impatient. The sun was shining, there was a slight breeze and it was hotter than normal for the end of June. A perfect day to go look for more dirt bike hills. It would be a great way to celebrate the first day of summer vacation, but instead we were spending it cooped up in Frank's cramped shop.

"Well?" I asked when he hung up.

Frank sighed. "It can't be done."

A man finds a way, Wes.

"Why not?"

"No parts."

"There have to be parts. Things break. They make extras."

Frank just shook his head. "Not making them anymore. Switching to digital signals. Analog towers are history."

There was silence as Zach and I took that in.

"What does that mean?" I asked finally.

"No more analog towers. No more rabbit ears."

I didn't like the sound of that.

Zach turned to me. "You'll just have to think of some other way to pay back your debt."

Frank looked at me. "What debt?"

My face flushed. I didn't really want the whole cane-shawl-afghan thing getting around, but I figured I could trust Frank. He barely talked to anyone.

"A life debt," I said.

"You're going to pay back a life debt by fixing a TV tower?"

"Well, it's not like I've got a lot of options. She's not being held by bandits. She's not tied to some railway tracks with a train coming. She's not surrounded by a pack of wolves or anything. She's getting up there in years, she's sick and she wants to see her granddaughter's ski race more than anything else in the world right now. She'd watch at a friend's, but her doctors say she can't leave her house."

"Why doesn't she just stream it on a computer?" Frank asked.

"She doesn't even have cable. Do you really think she has the Internet?"

"So take her a laptop. Someone must have one."

I wondered if Frank remembered how far into the boonies Six Roads was.

"There's no Wi-Fi near her house."

"Oh. Right."

"I can't think of any other way to repay her," I said.

Frank didn't answer right away, but then he nodded as if he understood about owing Mrs. Minton.

I waited, hope surging back.

"Gimme a couple of days. I got some connections."

I couldn't figure out what kind of connections you could have in the parts world. Was there a black market for toaster elements or something? But whatever it meant…I still had a chance.

"Here, take these cinnamon buns to Mrs. Minton, if you've got nothing better to do," my mom said. She had obviously had enough of my pacing. Waiting for Frank to call was harder than I thought. I kept checking to see if the phone was still working.

Mrs. Minton struggled to sit up when I came in. Her face was pale and her hand trembled as she reached for her glasses. How could someone change so much in so little time?

"Any news on the TV tower?" were the first words out of her mouth.

I gulped. Should I make something up just to make her feel better, or should I tell her the truth?

"Spit it out, Wesley."

The truth it was.

"Frank's looking into it."

"You mean he can't fix it." She lay back with a sigh and closed her eyes.

"I mean he's tracking down the parts he needs. Then he'll fix it," I said with more confidence than I felt.

She opened one eye. "He really thinks he can fix it?" With a great effort, she heaved herself back up into a sitting position.

"Sure he does. He just needs the parts."

"Do you think he'll be done in time for me to see Rachel's race? It's less than two weeks away." Her cheeks were flushed, and for the first time in a long time I saw the old spark in her eyes.

"Absolutely."

I prayed all the way home that I wasn't lying. *A man always tells it like it is, Wes.* Well, if I had any say in the matter, that's how it would be. I was going to do whatever it took to get that tower fixed so Mrs. Minton could watch her granddaughter's race.

Chapter 8

On Wednesday morning, Zach and I ran over to Frank's shop. After convincing him again that I wasn't going to sell my comic, I asked about the transmitter.

"Well, I got good news and bad news," he said.

I hate the good news-bad news game. If you chose the bad news first, the good news was never good enough to make up for it. And if you chose the good news first, you knew you couldn't enjoy it because somehow the bad news would cancel it out.

"Good news," Zach said, deciding for me.

"Good news is I found a used transmitter." He paused. "Bad news is, the guy doesn't want to sell it."

"Why won't he sell it?" I asked.

"Didn't really say."

"Did you tell him we'll pay top dollar for it?" Zach said. My stomach dropped. Top dollar? We didn't have top dollar. We barely had any dollars.

"I don't think he's interested in the money."

"Is there any way we can get it?" Zach asked, always practical.

"Well, I got good news and bad news."

I folded my arms.

"Good news, he's willing to trade for it. Bad news, it's in Pensacola, Florida."

I did some fast figuring in my head. It was about a six-day drive to Florida and back. I knew, because Dad and I drove to Disneyworld when I was nine. That would still give us time to have the transmitter installed before Rachel's World Championship race. Barely.

I smiled. "We'll take it."

"Whoa there," Zach said. "Trade it for what?" he asked Frank.

I'd forgotten about that part. What would a guy in Florida want from us?

Frank hesitated. That was a bad sign.

"He wants…um…winter."

Winter? Did I hear him right? "What do you mean, he wants winter?"

Frank sighed. "He's originally from Edmonton. He said it's his granddaughter's sixth birthday next week and he wants to build a snowman with her. Maybe have a snowball fight. She's never even seen snow, let alone played in it."

"Call him back and tell him it's hot here. You know, beach hot, sunburn hot, air-conditioning hot," I said, my voice rising just a little. "Is he one of those jerks who think we live in igloos all year round?"

"If he's from Edmonton, he knows that's not true, right?" Zach asked Frank, one eyebrow raised.

"I kind of got the feeling he was just jerking me around," Frank said, "but a deal is a deal. He said he would trade it for snow."

My heart sank.

"Well, tell him we'll give him snow in December. Tons of snow," Zach said.

"Yeah. I told him that. He said you can have the transmitter in December…if he still has it."

I groaned.

"Snow in summer. What a joke," Zach muttered.

Something twigged in the back of my mind.

"How big a snowman does he want to build?" I asked.

"What difference does that make?" Zach asked. "We don't have snow in July!"

"Sure we do," I answered, trying not to sound smug. "It's about twenty-five minutes away...at the Harrington Arena."

I could see the lightbulb go off in Zach's brain, and I knew he was thinking what I was thinking. The Zamboni! When the ice was cleared, there was always a small pile of snow left behind that had to be shoveled up.

"I dunno how much he wants," Frank said. "Enough for a snowman and a snowball fight before it all melts."

"Then snow he'll get," I said. "Call him back and tell him to get that transmitter ready. We'll take care of the snow."

Frank chuckled and reached for the phone.

Chapter 9

"Hey, we're in luck. The door is open," Zach said. The bus ride to the Harrington Arena had taken half an hour. I hadn't even considered that the arena might be locked up. We *were* lucky. According to a flyer on the door, there was a Junior B hockey camp going on.

"Yeah. At least we can get in," I said.

"More importantly, they'll be using the Zamboni," Zach said.

We walked around to where the Zamboni was parked, but no one was there. Down the hall was a maintenance room where you could get your skates sharpened. Inside, a man sat at an old wooden table drinking coffee and reading the paper. His hair was silver, and his blue overalls had the name *Bill* embroidered on the pocket.

"Dressing rooms are on the other side," he said without even looking up.

"Uh, thanks," I said. "But we're not here for the camp."

He put down his coffee and paper.

Might as well get right down to it. I never was any good at small talk.

"We were wondering if we could have some… well…um…snow." I let the words hang in the air.

"Snow." It was more a statement than a question.

"Yeah, you know, from the Zamboni."

"This some kind of joke?"

"No, sir. It's actually really important."

"Important to have snow from a Zamboni."

"It's hard to explain."

He got up. "Sorry, it's against the rules." He walked out before I could even think of something to say to convince him.

This was too much. First we found snow in summer, and then we couldn't have any.

Zach and I walked back out to the rink, stood at the boards and watched the Zamboni clear the ice. I couldn't believe we had come this close, only to fail.

"You guys here for the hockey camp?" one of the coaches called out to us as he skated over. "Or are you Chiefs fans?"

"No, not hockey camp. But we are big fans," Zach said. "My dad and I come to a lot of the Chiefs' hockey games. Do you think you're going to take the Sutherland Cup this year?"

The coach folded his arms and tilted his head. "Hard to say. Lots of competition. If this hockey camp is any indication, though, then we've got the talent. No doubt about it." He sighed. "But last year's heartbreaker in the finals got to us. Game seven and a tied score. Thirty-four seconds left in regulation play and a freak rebound off our guy's skate puts it in the net for them."

I sucked in my breath. That was a lousy way to go out.

"They'll bounce back this year," I said, trying to sound more optimistic than I felt. After all, I wasn't exactly having a good run of luck lately myself.

"You know, it's funny," the coach said. "A team can be the strongest, the fastest, the most talented, but if they don't believe they can win, they won't. It's that simple. I've seen it happen over and over again. Thing is, that's two years in a row we've lost in game seven with some bad luck. The Chiefs think they're jinxed."

The Zamboni had finished and was heading out the exit. Zach and I couldn't help groaning when we saw Bill shovel perfectly good, frozen, cold snow into a grate in the arena floor.

"We better get going, Wes," Zach said. "The bus to Six Roads leaves in about eight minutes."

"You guys are from Six Roads?"

"Yeah," I said as we turned to go.

The coach stopped me. "Isn't that where that guy found the lucky arrowhead?"

"Sure. Why?"

The coach rubbed his chin with this hand. "I know this sounds crazy, but that might be just what the team needs."

"An old arrowhead?"

"Yeah, like a lucky charm."

"I don't think it really is lucky."

"Doesn't matter."

"What do you mean?" I asked.

"All that matters is that the team thinks it's lucky. I could talk Bill into burying it at center ice like they did with that loonie at the Winter Olympics."

"Good luck talking Bill into anything," Zach muttered under his breath.

"Tell you what, Coach," I said, trying to keep the excitement out of my voice. "If you can get Bill to let us have some snow from the Zamboni, we'll get you that lucky arrowhead."

"Snow from the Zamboni?"

I sighed. "It's a long story. Do we have a deal?"

The coach smiled and held out his hand. "Deal. Sutherland Cup, here we come!"

Chapter 10

All the confidence I had felt back at the Harrington Arena a few hours before fizzled away as I stood on Mr. Elliot's porch.

"Well, are you going to knock?" Zach asked.

"Why don't *you* knock?" I said. "This whole life-debt thing was your idea."

Zach looked at the door and gulped. "And have him bark at me? No way."

I wanted to leave and forget the whole thing, but then I remembered how frail and sick Mrs. Minton was. I took a deep breath and knocked. We could hear footsteps coming to the door, and with each step my heart beat faster. I breathed again when Mrs. Elliot opened the door.

"Yes?" she said. She was a small, cheerful woman—the exact opposite of her husband. Mr. Elliot stayed on the farm like a hermit, but Mrs. Elliot was a member of every club in Six Roads—the sewing guild, the women's auxiliary for the church, the cheese sculptors. You name it, she was part of it.

"Uh, could we speak to Mr. Elliot, please?" I was secretly hoping she would say he wasn't home.

"Oh, Jack's out back doing some cleanup for me," she said, her smile growing wider.

"We wouldn't want to disturb him," I said hastily, the pit of dread growing in my stomach. "We'll come back some other time."

"Nonsense," she said. "I'm sure Jack would love a bit of company from you boys."

"Not likely," Zach whispered to me as we rounded the house.

But we were stuck now. Mrs. Elliot even said she was going to bring us some lemonade, as Jack would surely welcome a break. I was relieved that we wouldn't be left alone with him.

We could hear pounding as we neared the spot where Mr. Elliot was working. We stopped a few paces away, unsure what to do.

He must have heard us, because he swung around, sweat glistening on his forehead. "Well?"

My brain froze.

"We wanted to ask you a favor," I heard Zach say.

Mr. Elliot's eyes narrowed. "What kind of favor?"

"Would you let us have your arrowhead?" I blurted out. Like I said, I'm no good at small talk.

"Why?"

"To unjinx them," I stammered. "The team, I mean. The Chiefs." For some strange reason, my mouth was working, but my brain wasn't. Even *I* didn't understand what I was saying.

Mr. Elliot stared at me as if I had lost my mind.

Zach cleared his throat.

"Seeing as you don't believe in luck and the Chiefs do, and they need some, we wondered if you wouldn't mind donating your arrowhead to them," Zach said. Thank goodness his mouth and brain were connected.

"Yeah," I said weakly, wondering why I hadn't just let Zach do all the talking in the first place.

"Hmpfh." Mr. Elliot turned his back to us and kept piling rocks into a wheelbarrow.

Was that a "yes" hmpfh or a "no" hmpfh? We didn't know whether we should stay or go. We probably would have snuck away, but right then Mrs. Elliot came around the corner with a tray of lemonade and brownies. I can't resist brownies.

"Jack?"

"Hmm?"

"Jack, the boys are still waiting," she said.

Mr. Elliot turned around, his face unhappy. "I was just thinking about what they said."

Mrs. Elliot looked at him, her smile never fading.

"Why are you so interested in helping the Harrington Chiefs?" he asked us.

"It's not the Chiefs we want to help, it's Mrs. Minton," Zach said. Now I remembered why I didn't let him do all the talking. He was going to say too much, and the whole afghan episode would be tonight's dinner conversation all around town.

"Agnes Minton? She doesn't play hockey anymore."

"No, I mean we want to help her by fixing the TV tower."

"But the Harrington Chiefs' games aren't broadcast on TV, dear," Mrs. Elliot said gently.

"No ma'am, but by getting the arrowhead we'll get snow, which we're going to trade for a new transmitter to fix the tower to pay off Wes's life debt," Zach said.

I elbowed Zach.

Mrs. Elliot looked a little flustered. "Well, that sounds nice. Doesn't it, Jack?"

I almost felt a little sorry for Mr. Elliot. Mrs. Elliot was looking at him so sweetly. He must have been feeling kind of trapped.

Then his eyes glinted and a slow smile spread across his face. "Sure, I'll donate the arrowhead."

My stomach lurched. I knew that look only too well. When an adult looked at you like that, there was going to be a condition attached.

"And I'm sure the boys wouldn't mind helping me take down this old barn foundation in return."

Mrs. Elliot looked at us with eyes so bright you would think Mr. Elliot was offering us a week at summer camp instead of hours and hours of hard manual labor.

"Oh, I'm sure the boys wouldn't mind! They can start tomorrow." She beamed.

A man always respects his elders, Wes.

I groaned quietly. The old stone foundation was huge. Vines twisted and wound all over the rocks. It was going to take us forever.

"Well, now that that's settled, let's have some refreshment." Mrs. Elliot began pouring the lemonade.

This whole thing was getting horribly complicated.

Chapter 11

"What a way to spend summer vacation," Zach moaned. "Everyone else is going swimming at the quarry today."

I would have given anything to be jumping into the cool water too. Instead I was staring at a fortress of rocks and mortar that looked even bigger than it had on the day we got roped into pulling it down. Part of me just wanted to give up. Mrs. Minton probably didn't even remember what had happened at the creek. She was a kindhearted lady…she didn't really think I owed her a life debt, did she?

And now Mr. Elliot expected us to take down his foundation, we had promised the Chiefs' coach the arrowhead, and the guy in Florida was waiting for his snow. I groaned.

"What did Mr. Elliot tell us again?" I asked.

"One pile for the rocks. One pile for the mortar," Zach's imitation of Mr. Elliot was so perfect, I snorted.

Mr. Elliot had said he was going to a meeting in town. I thought he could have at least stayed to help us.

Zach grabbed the pickax and, with a grunt, swung it at the foundation. It bounced off and almost knocked him to the ground.

Next he took a crowbar and tried to wedge it in the crumbling mortar. He strained to pry the rock out but stopped after a few minutes, panting. I went over to help him. It still took almost ten minutes to finally free the stone, even with two of us putting all our weight into it. I picked it up and carried it to the pile.

"One down, thousands to go," Zach said.

I could feel the energy drain from my muscles.

"This is nuts," I said. "We'll never get this done in time to get that transmitter. Are you sure Mr. Elliot won't give us the arrowhead now if we promise to finish this later?"

"I'm sure." Zach threw back his shoulders to do another impression of Mr. Elliot. "'Young people are notoriously unreliable.'" That one had me rolling on the ground.

We tried to pry another rock out.

Zach threw down the crowbar in disgust.

A man works smarter, not harder, Wes.

"I've got an idea," I said.

"Does it involve shade, drinks and rest?"

"Yes."

"Count me in. What is it?"

"Daryl."

Silence.

"You know that Mr. Elliot hates him, right?" Zach finally said.

"He won't even know he was here."

"Somehow those sound like famous last words."

We left Mr. Elliot's place and biked over to Daryl's. He was just coming out of his workshop when we cornered him and told him our plan. At first he seemed interested, but the minute he heard Mr. Elliot's name he started to sweat and shake his head.

"It's for a really good cause," I said in my best wheedling voice.

"No, no, no, no, no, no," Daryl said, backing away with his hands up in surrender.

"Come on, Daryl. You're the only one who can help us," Zach said.

Daryl shifted nervously. You could see him struggle between his fear of Mr. Elliot and the thrill of blowing something up. "You sure Mr. Elliot isn't there?"

"He went into Harrington for a co-op meeting. Those things run two hours at least," I said.

"What about Mrs. Elliot?" Daryl asked, licking his lips nervously.

"Her book club meets today."

"I don't know," Daryl said slowly. "Mr. Elliot said if he ever saw me near his place again he'd"—he blushed—"he'd put my explosives somewhere uncomfortable."

"He's all talk," I said. "I think that he'd be grateful to have that foundation down so quickly."

Zach nodded vigorously.

Daryl finally agreed. I think the idea that he might actually be doing something to please old Jack was what really turned the tide in our favor. Daryl didn't like the idea of being hated by anyone. What was one flying cow between neighbors?

We waited impatiently while Daryl filled a canvas shoulder bag with stuff from his workshop. I didn't see exactly what went in there, but it looked heavy.

Daryl gave a low whistle when he saw the foundation and all the vines. In a flash he whipped out his tape measure and climbed all over the pile, taking measurements and talking to himself. It seemed to take forever.

Zach kept glancing over at me with this panicked look on his face as the minutes ticked by. I was starting to get that sick feeling in my stomach.

"If Mr. Elliot comes back and sees Daryl, well, you can kiss that arrowhead goodbye," Zach whispered.

I didn't want to admit it, but Zach was right. If we couldn't get the arrowhead, it would be the end of our plan. Still, Daryl was the reason we were in this mess in the first place. Wasn't it only right that he be the one to help us fix it?

Daryl finally trotted over to us with a look on his face like a puppy who has found a chew toy under the couch.

"Easy as falling off a log," he told us.

"Well, get to it, Daryl," I said, feeling nervous. "Before Mr. Elliot gets back."

At the mention of Mr. Elliot's name, Daryl's eyes opened wide. "Oh, yeah," he said, trotting back to the wall with his bag.

I tried really hard not to fidget as he took his time placing the blasting caps in and around the inner base of the wall. Sometimes he'd remeasure something and then move the explosive what looked like a quarter inch. All the while my stomach was churning. I hadn't thought it would take this long. I had pictured Daryl simply stacking some dynamite all around the wall and blasting it to bits.

"Daryl!" I yelled. "I don't think moving it that little bit will make any difference. Come on! Hurry up!"

Daryl stood up and gave me his version of a stern look. "If these sticks aren't placed right, those stones are gonna go flying in every direction, twenty, maybe thirty, feet. Do you want one flying through the kitchen window or knocking out one of Mr. Elliot's cows over there?" He jerked his head in the direction of the cow pasture not fifteen feet away. Esmeralda looked up at the sound of his voice. She backed away from the fence.

Daryl bent back down, shaking his head and muttering under his breath.

"Daryl's right," Zach said. "Those rocks could go anywhere."

My head started to ache. I hadn't even thought about stuff getting damaged. I just wanted those rocks loose so we could pile them up. It was time to call this off. Mr. Elliot was due home any minute.

When we turned around, Daryl wasn't by the wall anymore. He waved to us from behind Mr. Elliot's shed. There was a little black box in his hand and a happy smile on his face. We raced over to him.

"Forget this, Daryl!" I panted. "Just take it all back and I'll make this up to you."

Daryl looked confused and hurt. "But it's all ready. One press of this button and we're done."

I opened my mouth to say "No!" and then everything warped into slow motion again as disaster loomed. I tried to wave Daryl off as he smiled and moved his hand to the button. I heard the crunch of tires on gravel and the slam of a truck door. And then *BOOM!*

Chapter 12

It took me a couple of minutes to realize that I was flat on my back looking up at the sky. The puffy clouds looked so peaceful drifting along, you wouldn't have thought that a world war was about to erupt.

"What in the world have you done now!?" I had never heard Mr. Elliot at full volume before, and I have to admit, even with my ears ringing a little from the blast, it was impressive. I could feel the ground shake as he stormed over to us. I figured for safety's sake, I should get up.

I was still a little woozy, but a quick check convinced me that all I had was a small bump on my head. The shed had protected us from the worst of the blast. Zach was struggling to get up beside me. I couldn't see Daryl.

Mr. Elliot reached us in what seemed like two strides. A huge vein throbbed in his neck, and his eyes bulged. I was so terrified, I couldn't even speak.

Mrs. Elliot came up behind him. "Now, Jack," she said calmly, "I'm sure the boys are fine."

The look in Mr. Elliot's eyes told me that he wasn't as relieved as she was that we were both okay. I think he was from the old school, where young boys who had crazy ideas got what they deserved. I was never so grateful to see Mrs. Elliot in all my life.

Mr. Elliot's teeth were clamped together so tightly that the words could barely escape his mouth. "What. Happened?"

It would have taken one of Daryl's sticks of dynamite to get me to open my mouth right then.

Luckily Zach found his voice. "We were just trying to find a way to speed the job up. So we called in some help." His eyes were wide and pleading for mercy from Mrs. Elliot.

"Oh no." A look of horror spread over Mr. Elliot's face as he realized what Zach meant by "help." "Daryl," he whispered.

Right on cue, Daryl's head popped up from the spot where the foundation had been.

Mr. Elliot walked over to him very slowly. It was actually scarier than if he had run. Daryl didn't move.

"It was perfect," Daryl said with a quiver in his voice. "See?" He pointed to the area behind him. Zach, Mrs. Elliot and I ran over.

The foundation was gone. The stones and mortar had all collapsed inward, leaving a neat pile of rubble. None of the stones had scattered, and nothing was damaged. It was amazing.

"You," was all Mr. Elliot managed to say.

"Well, look at that, Jack," Mrs. Elliot said, smiling. "What a neat and tidy job Daryl made of this. Why didn't you think of that?"

Mr. Elliot was speechless.

"Daryl," Mrs. Elliot said, taking his arm and walking him back to the house, "have you ever thought about going into the demolition business? I know Mr. Palmer over Dunkirk way wants to have his old silo taken down."

I couldn't hear Daryl's answer, and I suddenly realized that we were alone with Mr. Elliot. Zach and I froze. I hoped he wouldn't remember we were there. He wasn't looking at us though. He was staring at Daryl's handiwork.

As if on cue, we both took a silent step backward, praying we could escape.

He turned to us as if to say something, but no words came out. He looked back at the rubble. We moved back another step.

It was like a bad game of Red Light, Green Light.

"STOP!"

Game over.

"I…You…This…He…" Mr. Elliot sputtered like a lawnmower out of gas. He took a deep breath. "Two piles," he barked. "I want this stuff in two piles by tomorrow."

Chapter 13

Zach and I felt pretty good as we walked to Lee's the next day. We had finished piling all of Mr. Elliot's rocks and mortar, and I had the arrowhead in my pocket. Tomorrow we planned to take the arrowhead to the Chiefs' coach and make arrangements to get our snow. Everything was falling into place.

We thought we'd stop in at Frank's shop to tell him the good news. He was in his usual spot at his computer.

"So we figure if you leave tomorrow, we could have the transmitter here by, say, next Thursday," I told Frank. "Do you think you could start installing it next Friday?" I was eager to get this whole thing over with.

Frank laced his hands on his chest as he rocked back in his chair.

"Problem," he said.

Surely he wasn't going to tell us he couldn't do it because there was a hair-dryer repair workshop next week or something.

"Yours or ours?" Zach asked. He was always pretty good about getting to the bottom of things.

"Yours."

So, no workshop.

"What problem?" I asked.

"Getting the snow down there and the transmitter up here."

He was right. I'd been concentrating so hard on getting the transmitter and the snow and the arrowhead that I'd completely forgotten to figure out a way to make the trade. I had to think fast.

"Zach and I will check out the bus and train schedules and get some camping coolers for the snow," I said.

Frank shook his head but didn't say anything.

"What?" Sometimes trying to talk to Frank made my teeth ache.

Frank leaned forward on his desk. "Snow'll never make it all that way in a cooler."

I opened my mouth to argue with him, but he was right. When we went camping, we had to load up on ice every day or so in the hot weather. And a block of ice lasts way longer than a pile of snow.

"And"—Frank wasn't done yet—"who's gonna let two eleven-year-olds go down there alone?"

I closed my mouth. I hate it when people who think they're smarter than me actually turn out to be smarter than me. I tried to think of a quick solution, but nothing came to mind. How *were* we going to get the snow to Florida and bring the transmitter back?

Something inside of me snapped. This whole thing was spiraling out of control. There probably was no such thing as a life debt. Zach was just pulling my leg. And even if there was such a thing, there was no proof that Mrs. Minton had ever heard of it. Or expected me to repay one. I very seriously doubted that she was sitting (or lying, I guess) in her living room thinking I owed her something.

Everyone else was having fun on their summer vacations, and here I was chasing down snow, arrowheads and transmitters. And for what? No one was going to come after me if I didn't do this. Heck, no one even expected an eleven-year-old to be responsible for fixing this. Adults should be doing this. Adults like Frank. Or even Daryl.

I wanted to argue with Frank, but I knew he was right.

"I'm done," I said.

"What?" Zach asked.

"Frank is right. This whole thing is stupid." I walked out of the shop.

Zach didn't come after me. I was kind of glad. I didn't really feel like talking to anyone.

A man sees things through, Wes.

I pushed thoughts of my dad out of my head.

Chapter 14

The next day was sunny and warm. A perfect summer day. Now that I was free, I wondered what to do first. Game Box? Movies? Checking out dirt bike trails? Just hanging out? It was hard to say. I couldn't make up my mind, so I headed to Lee's for some junk food. A heavy dose of sugar would help me decide.

I didn't call Zach. The whole life debt nonsense had been his idea, so maybe he was a bit mad at me for blowing it off.

There was a low rumble under my feet. Daryl. It was pretty far away though. I guess he was trying to keep a low profile.

A blast of air-conditioning hit me as I went into the store. Mr. Lee was hanging a banner, that read *Happy Anniversary*.

"Whose anniversary is it?" I asked him.

"Ours," he said, smiling. "We been here ten years this month."

"Wow. Congratulations."

"Here, you deserve special deal on chips and pop. One dollar."

"Great! But why me?"

"Without your father, it would not be possible. We would not be here at all."

"My dad?"

"Sure. He helped me big-time to buy business. The old owner left town without giving us the survey. The bank said we couldn't get a mortgage without it. Your dad"—he shook his head in admiration—"he tracked down the owner. For weeks. He called his boss, his neighbors. He drove eighty miles away to find him. He never stopped until he found him."

I smiled and nodded, but inside, my gut was churning. I left the store, dragging my feet.

A man never gives up, Wes.

My dad didn't just say the words, he lived them. And what was I doing? Running away as soon as things got tough. Pathetic.

I was so lost in thought that I almost smacked into Zach outside of Lee's.

"Hey, Wes. You okay?"

Relief washed over me. Zach wasn't mad.

I didn't know where to begin. "Sorry. I kinda snapped yesterday. I just got, you know, frustrated."

Zach shrugged. "So, are we still gonna do this?"

"I guess so. I just don't know how."

"Maybe this will help." Zach walked over to the hose by the pumps and jumped on it. The bells chimed.

He looked up and grinned.

I didn't know what to say. My friend had clearly lost his mind.

"Gee, that's great, Zach. Why don't we get you out of the hot sun?"

Zach's only response was to jump on the hose again, still grinning.

"Don't you get it?" he asked.

"Get what?"

"Where'd Mr. Lee get the bells for this?"

"Uh, the *Nice 'n Icy* truck out back?" I humored him as I tried to steer him into the air-conditioned store.

"Yes! The *Nice 'n Icy* truck that's REFRIGERATED," he said triumphantly.

Of course! A refrigerated truck would keep the snow from melting! Why hadn't I thought of that?

"All we need now is a driver," I said.

Frank was tinkering with someone's waffle maker while we sat on his desk trying to solve our new problems, which were a) did the ice-cream truck still run? b) would Mr. Lee let us borrow it? and c) who would drive it all the way to Florida and back?

There was no way we would be allowed to go. We had both already asked, and we were both told "absolutely not." I had worked on my mom for over half an hour, but no matter what angle I tried, the answer was the same. Life debt or no life debt, I was not going to Florida. And anyway, I couldn't drive.

As we sat on Frank's desk, I caught Zach's eye. We had been friends long enough that we always knew what the other guy was thinking, and we both knew that the answer was right in front of us. Frank. Frank could fix the truck if it needed it, he was good friends with Mr. Lee and, more importantly, he had his driver's license. We didn't quite know how to ask, though, so we just kept looking at each other and shrugging.

"I'm not going," Frank said without even turning around to face us. How did he know we were going to ask him?

"You're our only hope, Frank," I said. I meant it.

"This is your problem, not mine. I didn't almost drown in the creek."

"Well, I guess that's it then," I said. "Mrs. Minton will have to miss Rachel's race. If she even lasts that long."

"Oh no you don't. Don't you pull that guilt trip on me," Frank said, spinning around.

What can I say? After years of having Mom guilt-trip me, I was an expert.

Frank put down the waffle maker. "Look. I got a business to run. I can't just take off for a week to drive an ice-cream truck down the highway. I got bills to pay."

"We'll pay you," I said suddenly. Zach's mouth dropped open.

"What do you mean, we'll pay him?" he asked. "Where are we going to find the money to pay him? My allowance barely covers snacks at Lee's and the occasional comic book."

"Then we'll pay him some other way. Work for him for free or something."

Frank went back to his waffle maker. "I don't need any help."

There was this little itch at the back of my brain, like I knew the answer to this and just didn't want to remember it.

"How about running deliveries for you?" I said. "Or doing your laundry? Or your whole family's laundry?"

"Nope."

The itch got bigger. I knew how to pay Frank. But just the thought of it made me feel sick. But in my mind, I saw Mrs. Minton's face—strong and determined when she pulled me out of the creek, and pale and tired as she lay on her bed.

People are more important than things, Wes.

"How about if I give you my Spider-Man comic?" I didn't mean it to come out in a whisper.

Frank whirled around, a look of astonishment on his face. "Are you kidding? Issue number four, where he meets Doctor Octopus? You'd really give it to me if I drive to Florida?"

I tried not to gulp out loud as I said, "Yup."

Zach grabbed my arm. "Are you sure, Wes?"

"Yeah. I'm sure." I tried not to sound sad when I said it. "So will you do it?"

"You really gonna give up your chance at a dirt bike for old Mrs. Minton?" Frank asked.

"A man pays his debts," I mumbled.

"That's the craziest thing I ever heard," Frank said. "But I'd be even crazier not to take it. That issue will complete my collection, you know." He sounded like a kid, not a grown man with a soldering gun.

"Yeah, I know. So you'll do it?"

He paused, as if he wasn't sure if I was serious or not. "All right. Get me some snow and a map."

I had to smile, despite the fact that I would never feel the wind and dust on my face as I sped across the fields and over jumps on my 250cc Hummer.

Chapter 15

I thought time had crawled by when I was waiting for summer vacation to start, but that was nothing compared to waiting while Frank drove down to Florida and back.

Zach and I had agreed to look after Frank's shop while he was away, taking in work and answering the phone. I would have preferred to be swimming at the quarry or having a video game marathon, but it seemed only right that we help Frank out.

Frank said he would email us from his iPhone. We checked the computer in the shop every half an hour for a day until finally the first email came.

Rough road. Spilled coffee. Need new pants.

It didn't sound like a good beginning to the trip.

"Didn't he take another pair of pants?" Zach asked. "He really should have got some good travel clothes. I saw this documentary on traveling in Africa once, where this guy's hat was eaten by an elephant. A few days later he found it in a pile of, well, you know what. He washed it out and it was as good as new."

I should've been grossed out, but it was pretty funny. "Did that really happen?" I asked, wondering if Zach was pulling my leg.

"Yup." Zach's face was totally serious. "I think it's on the hat company's website now."

I hoped Frank wasn't planning on being around any elephants.

Just before we left the shop for the day, Frank sent another email. *17-mile detour. No motels. Sleeping in truck.*

I tried not to feel too guilty that night as I lay in my soft bed in clean pajamas. But then I spied my Spider-Man comic in its plastic cover, and I didn't feel so bad.

The next morning, Zach opened the shop while I went over to give Mrs. Minton an update.

"Frank's on his way to get the transmitter," I told her.

"Is there going to be enough time?" Mrs. Minton asked, worry etched on her face. "The race is in five days."

"Sure," I said, trying to ooze confidence.

"What about the tower? Is it fixed yet?"

I didn't answer right away. I'd been so obsessed with getting the transmitter, I'd totally forgotten about the tower.

"Not quite done yet," I said. Inside, I was panicking. How dumb was that? What good was a transmitter if there was no tower or antenna?

What could I tell her that wasn't a lie? I didn't know how I could possibly get a ninety-foot tower fixed and upright in five days.

A man isn't afraid to ask for help, Wes.

"You don't happen to know anyone with a really tall ladder, do you?" I joked. Well, I was only half joking. It was going to take something really tall to lift that tower back into position.

I could feel Mrs. Minton's eyes on me. I looked at the ground.

"I wonder if Steve could help," she said.

"Steve?"

"Steve Anderson. He works for Harrington Hydro."

"Why would someone from Hydro help me?"

"As a favor to me, I guess," she said. "I helped Steve train for the World Karate Championship a few years ago. He won a silver medal. Now he has that nice tall bucket truck. I'm sure if I asked him, he'd be happy to help."

I'm sure I looked stunned. Mrs. Minton taught karate? Was there anything she couldn't do?

As good as her word, Mrs. Minton arranged for Steve and his crew to go over and fix the tower the next day. I went over and saw them hammer the bent pieces straight and try to fit it all together again. It was a bit like a jigsaw puzzle. I hoped that it wouldn't take too long. Mr. Anderson assured me that if they didn't finish by nightfall, it would be done by the next day. I thanked him and then left, hoping I didn't owe *him* some kind of debt now too.

The next day was pretty quiet at the shop. *Windshield cracked by turkey vulture* was the next message from Frank. I didn't know what to make of that. I was starting to feel very glad I had stayed home.

Tornado warning came next.

I was starting to wish we weren't getting updates.

The next one made my stomach ache. It said simply *Lost*.

"He's never going to make it, is he?" Zach asked.

Day three had us hovering around the computer, afraid to look. Had Frank made it or not? We didn't hear about any tornadoes touching down or hijackings of ice-cream trucks, but we still worried.

When we did get up the nerve to check, the mailbox was empty.

Finally, just after lunch, another email.

"Well, did he get the transmitter or not?" I asked Zach who was on the computer.

"Doesn't say. Just says, *Arrived*."

"I guess that's good news, right?"

"I guess," Zach said, but he didn't sound all that convinced.

Day four: *Baby on board.*

"Please tell me he means the transmitter and not a real baby," I said to Zach.

"I dunno. With the kind of trip he's been having, that could mean anything."

Day five: *Construction. Taking shortcut.*

"That doesn't sound like a good idea," Zach said.

Then: *Delay from shortcut. Enjoyed Pittsburgh.*

"Pittsburgh? What's he doing in Pittsburgh?" I asked.

"We're never going to see him again, are we?" Zach replied.

Against all odds, we did see him again. He rolled back into town on day five, the ice-cream truck belching black smoke and making strange rattling sounds. He opened the door to his shop, walked past us straight to his desk chair, sat down, put his head in his arms and fell asleep.

We went back to check on Frank after a couple of hours, but he was gone. I hoped he was resting, because we needed to get started on that transmitter right away. We were running out of time. The race was in two days.

Chapter 16

I was so impatient to get that transmitter hooked up and working that I ran all the way to Frank's shop the next morning.

He wasn't there, and the shop wasn't open. Had he skipped town? I shook my head. Frank wouldn't desert us. Besides, I hadn't given him the comic book yet. Come to think of it, he hadn't given us the transmitter either. I hadn't even seen it. Frank must have left it on the truck.

I went around back to check for the truck. It wasn't there.

Frank must already be working on the tower. Good old Frank. I jogged over to Daryl's place so I could see how things were coming along. I even grabbed a cold root beer at Lee's for Frank.

As the hill came into view, I was surprised to see the tower deserted. No truck, no Frank, no transmitter.

I turned back, confused. If the truck wasn't behind Frank's shop or here at the tower, where was it?

I took off to get Zach. Things were starting to get complicated again.

"Morning, Wes," Zach's mother said when I knocked on the back door. "Go on up and get him. It's about time he was up anyway."

I took the steps two at a time. Zach must have heard me coming, because he met me at his door, his eyes still groggy with sleep.

"Zach! The truck's gone!"

Zach rubbed his eyes with the back of his hand "We don't own a truck."

I hit him on the shoulder. "No! The ice-cream truck!"

"Oh yeah. That truck. Um, I guess Frank's getting a head start."

"That's just it," I said. "He's not at the tower."

Zach looked like his brain was stuck in neutral. "So where is he?"

I could feel disaster lurking just around the corner. I don't know why, but I had a bad feeling about the truck.

A man trusts his gut, Wes.

"We have to find Frank and that truck," I said. "Now."

"All right," he mumbled, throwing on some clothes and grabbing his cap. "Let's go."

We tore over to Frank's shop. Part of me thought maybe I was just hallucinating before. Maybe the truck was sitting there after all. It wasn't.

"The truck's not here," Zach said.

"Thanks for clearing that up, Zach."

"I'm just saying." He looked kind of hurt. "Let's ask Mr. Lee. It's his truck, after all."

We found Mr. Lee filling the rack of air fresheners by the oil display.

"Mr. Lee, have you seen Frank?"

"Frank in store. He fix cash register for Mrs. Lee."

"Do you know where the *Nice 'n Icy* truck is?"

Mr. Lee smiled. "Sure. I lend it to my cousin. He go to warehouse for me."

"Did you take the transmitter out?"

"The what?"

"The transmitter," I said. "The thing Frank went all the way to Florida to get?"

"I don't know about no transmitter. I didn't take anything out."

I was speechless. The transmitter we had gone through so much to get was barreling down the highway in the opposite direction from where it was needed. I looked at Zach in horror.

"We'll find it in time, Wes," Zach said.

"We'll need wheels to find it," I said. "With room for a transmitter."

"Mr. Elliot has a truck," Zach offered.

Mr. Lee shook his head. "Mr. Elliot taking load of stones up north. Some crazy lady wants to make pond with them."

Daryl.

Daryl had a truck. And besides, I still blamed him for all of this.

Mr. Lee said he would go and get Frank. Zach and I would go get Daryl and his truck and come back to Lee's. All I needed now was for Daryl to be off somewhere blowing something up. But finally some luck was with us. Daryl's truck was parked in his driveway, and Daryl himself was just coming out the front door.

"No, no, no and no!" he said before I could even explain to him why we were there. Obviously he was still upset with us about that last little episode with Mr. Elliot.

"Just listen, Daryl," I said.

"No. I'm not listening. You're nothing but trouble."

Okay, that was a bit much. Daryl calling someone else trouble.

"We just need a lift, Daryl," I said. "Everyone else's truck is being used. You're our last hope."

Daryl tilted his head to one side. "Just a lift?"

"Yeah."

"Where to?"

"Uh, we just need to find an ice-cream truck," I said.

Daryl folded his arms. "You guys are just foolin' with me, aren't you?"

You know, I couldn't blame him. It sounded ridiculous, even to me. Blowing up foundations, getting snow in the summer and chasing down runaway ice-cream trucks. Who wouldn't think this was a joke?

"I know it sounds crazy, Daryl," I said. "But we really need the transmitter that's inside that truck. It's for Mrs. Minton. It's practically a matter of life and death."

That last bit might have been a bit of a stretch, but I knew there was no way Daryl was going to let himself be responsible for old Mrs. Minton's health. He was in.

We picked up Frank at Lee's and headed down the highway, scanning the horizon for the *Nice 'n Icy* truck.

"There it is," Frank said calmly, pointing up ahead.

"Where? Where?" I asked. I couldn't see anything. The highway curved out of sight.

"See that cloud of black smoke?" Frank asked.

I could just make out a dark gray smudge hanging above the road up ahead.

"That's it. I'd know that smoke anywhere."

Sure enough, as we sped up and rounded the curve, we saw the *Nice 'n Icy* truck limping along in the slow lane, spouting gray smoke.

"That thing should be put out of its misery," Daryl muttered. His eyes glinted.

"There's nothing wrong with that truck that can't be fixed with the right parts," Frank said, a bit of tension in his voice.

It suddenly occurred to me that I was sandwiched in the cab of a pickup between one guy who lived to blow things up and another who lived to fix them. And they were both eyeing the truck. It made me more than a little uneasy. I didn't want to be in the middle of a fight.

A man keeps the peace, Wes.

How was I going to prevent a world war without getting caught in the crossfire?

"Well, it's Mr. Lee's truck," I said, "so I guess he gets to decide what to do with it."

"Bah," said Daryl on my left.

"Hmpfh," said Frank on my right.

We pulled up beside the truck and waved it over.

It took a lot of explaining and reassurance to convince Mr. Lee's cousin that Mr. Lee had sent us and that we needed to get something out of the back of the truck. It would have been simpler if Mr. Lee had come with us, but he had to stay and sign for a delivery of toilet plungers.

My first impression of the transmitter was disappointing. It was all crated up, and there seemed to be smoke coming off it.

"What's that?" I asked Frank. "Is it supposed to do that?

"Uh, I think it's frozen."

I couldn't even bring myself to ask if that was going to be a problem.

As we pulled back on the highway to drive back, I saw both Daryl and Frank look at the truck longingly.

We got back in record time, and as we pulled into the driveway, I turned to Frank. "So, you think you can start on this today? The race is Saturday."

"Yeah," Frank grunted. "Before anything else happens to it."

Chapter 17

It was a race against time now. We only had barely a day and a half. Frank worked on the transmitter for hours. I hung around the tower with him. I couldn't really help him. It was more for moral support.

I don't know why, but I had this crazy thought that you could just—you know—set it up and plug it in. Presto, TV channels. But it was more complicated than that. Circuits had to be connected, cables attached, antennae hooked up, stuff tuned, amplified and who knew what else.

It seemed to take forever before we were ready to test it. I stood by while Frank gave it a try.

Nothing happened. Was something supposed to *whir* or *clunk*? I looked at Frank's face, and that old feeling of doom washed over me.

"What's wrong now?" I asked.

"The bloody thing isn't compatible with our system."

"How can that be? You checked, didn't you?"

Frank flung the screwdriver to the ground so hard that it spun and stuck in. Any other time, it would have been really impressive.

"Of course I checked. But the transmitter and antennae are made by different companies. They're supposed to work together, but they don't."

"What now?" The words came out of me like the wail of an injured animal.

Frank didn't say anything for a minute while he stared at the transmitter.

"I'm not making any promises, but I think, with a couple of parts, I might be able to make it work."

I tried hard not to lose my cool. Besides, I had to get up enough courage to go and give an update to Mrs. Minton. I wasn't looking forward to it. The bike ride from Frank's back field to Mrs. Minton's would only have taken me about ten minutes on a good day. I dragged it out to twenty.

"Hello, Wesley," she said before I was barely in the door. I hadn't even taken my shoes off. "What news?"

I couldn't look her in the eye. "Frank's connecting everything."

It didn't work. She knew. "You said that earlier, Wesley. What's wrong?"

I sighed. There was no fooling Mrs. Minton.

"Just a small compatibility problem. Frank seems sure he can make it work."

She didn't answer for so long, I had to look up. She was staring at me.

"That bad, eh, Wesley? Well, if anyone can fix it..." She didn't finish the sentence, but it was obvious that, in her mind, Frank was a miracle worker. I just hoped she was right. The race was the next day.

"What time is Rachel's race?" I asked, trying to make it sound like an innocent question.

"We're cutting it that close, are we?"

I sighed.

"The race is being broadcast starting at two PM, but I don't know exactly when Rachel skis. They draw race order in the morning."

"We'll get it done, Mrs. Minton. Don't worry."

She smiled a weak smile and closed her eyes.

I stayed away from Frank the rest of the day. I couldn't do anything anyway.

The next morning, I went straight to the tower.

I could hear him muttering before I saw him.

"For the love of…Who in their right mind…Fit, darn it! Fit! I don't believe this!"

Sure didn't sound good.

"Hiya, Frank. How's it going? Can I get you anything?"

Frank's head popped up. "Oh, it's going just great." Sarcasm dripped off every word. "Two circuits aren't working at all, the bandwidth is all wrong, one arm of an antenna snapped, the power supply shorted out and I cut my finger."

He glared at me as if daring me to say something optimistic. Man, was I sorry I asked. I shrugged my shoulders, shook my head and made what I hoped were sympathetic hand gestures. I needed help. I ran for Zach. We only had about two and a half hours until the start of the race. At some point we had to face Mrs. Minton. I say "we" because this stupid life-debt idea was Zach's fault somehow, and he was going to suffer with me.

Zach and I sat on my porch for a while, too terrified to check on how Frank was making out and even more terrified to go to Mrs. Minton with bad news.

"Should we go see Frank?" Zach asked eventually. "There's only about half an hour until the race."

I wanted to snap back that I knew how to tell time too, but there was that voice.

A man faces the music, Wes.

I guess it was time I did that.

"Come on, Zach. Let's see Frank and get the verdict."

I can't even repeat the language we heard as we neared the tower. Well, at least we had our answer.

"Uh, Frank? You okay?"

Frank backed out of the housing and stood up. "If this wasn't for Mrs. Minton, I would have gotten Daryl to blow this up too."

I felt a heavy weight on my chest. How would I tell Mrs. Minton that we had failed?

"How bad is it?" asked the ever practical Zach.

"I've got everything patched up, except there's a break in this wire somewhere, and I'll be darned if I can find it." He was running the cable through both hands trying to feel for the break. "Now, if I stand on top of the transmitter housing and hold it like this"—he climbed up and held the cable over his head and out to the side a bit—"then I can get the signal. But the minute I let go"—he dropped his hand—"it's gone." He jumped down. "Why can't I find this break?" He was speaking more to himself now.

"About how long do you think you can stay in that position?" I asked.

Frank looked at me in horror as he realized what I was thinking. "Oh, no. You can't be serious!" He looked from me to Zach and back again. "You really expect me to stand up there with my arms in the air like some demented cheerleader?"

"It would only be for a couple of minutes. Just long enough for Mrs. Minton to see Rachel's run." Zach sounded so calm and logical that I knew he was reeling Frank in. "If you could only see how much this means to Mrs. Minton…"

Really, Zach was so good at this, I believed he had a future in politics. Maybe foreign affairs. The United Nations, even.

Frank banged his head a couple of times on the side of the transmitter housing like he couldn't believe that he was about to agree to this. "And how will I know when her race is starting, or when it's over?" he asked, resigned to his fate.

"I'll grab the walkie-talkies," I said, thinking on my feet so fast, even my dad would have been impressed. "If you give us little scans every two minutes or so, we can listen for the race order and let you know when we're getting close."

"Tell me this is all a bad dream," Frank said to the sky. I waited a second or two in case he got an answer. He sighed. "Go get the walkie-talkies then, and if there is any good karma owed to me at all, I'll find that break before I have to use them."

We took off. We had about ten minutes until the start of the race. I hoped Rachel wasn't up too near the beginning.

Zach volunteered to take the one walkie-talkie back to Frank while I raced over to Mrs. Minton's house with the other one.

When I got in the door, Mrs. Minton was just dabbing her eyes. The TV was on, and the screen was nothing but snow. And not the kind you find on a ski hill. The only sounds were static and the fan blowing cool air on Mrs. Minton's face.

"Be sure and thank Frank for trying," she said. "And you too, Wesley. I know you did everything you could." She dabbed her eyes again.

"We're not giving up yet," I told her, switching on the walkie-talkie. "But it is a long shot."

"Come in, Frank," I said into the unit. "Over."

There was a lot of crackling, then, "Frank here. Ready for test? Over."

"Ready. Over."

Zach burst through the door as the snow on the TV buzzed, wavered and a grainy picture came and went.

"Weak signal, Frank. I can't get a fix on the race. Over."

The picture came in again, but only in black and white.

"How's that? Over."

It flickered to color for a second.

"Zach, move those rabbit ears a bit. I think we can get it."

Zach fiddled with the antenna arms: up high, down low, in the middle.

"Stop!" I said. The picture had been clear for a second.

"Back around a bit, Zach."

"There!" Mrs. Minton said, seeing the starting gate and hearing the announcers voice come in. "Who did he say was on course?"

"I don't know," I said. "Does it look like Rachel?"

Mrs. Minton squinted at the screen. "No. Rachel's suit is yellow with red tiger stripes."

"Isn't that a yellow and red suit in the warm-up area?" Zach asked.

The walkie-talkie crackled.

"Can I get down now? Over." Frank sounded a bit stressed.

"Just a minute, Frank. We think Rachel is up soon. Over."

"How long is soon? Over."

We listened for the announcer. It was hard to make out because half the words were missing as we got and then lost the signal.

"...here at...next skier...'ian team...'chel Moore."

"That's her!" Mrs. Minton yelled.

"Hold on for a few more minutes, Frank. Rachel's up next. Over."

"Aaargh. Over."

Chapter 18

We could barely see the image of a yellow suit with red tiger stripes just behind the start gate.

Zach moved the base of the rabbit ears ever so slightly back and forth, trying to get any improvement in the picture.

I moved the antennae up and down by centimeters. When I thought it was pretty good, I let go and stepped back. The image turned to snow. When I touched the antenna again, the picture cleared.

Rachel was now in the start gate, poles over the bar, rocking back and forth. Then I heard *Beep. Beep. Beeeeeeeeep.*

"Now on course, Rachel Moore of Canada."

"Freeze!" Mrs. Minton yelled.

Zach was stepping away from the TV, both hands up like he was surrendering to it. I had one hand up touching the top of one antennae and one arm out to the side like I was directing a jumbo jet. We held our breath and prayed the picture would hold for the minute or so it would take Rachel to reach the bottom of the hill.

I dared to turn my head and look at Mrs. Minton.

She was sitting up in her bed, her eyes riveted on the screen. Her hands were in fists as if she were holding her own ski poles. As Rachel skidded around the corners, Mrs. Minton's body leaned with her. Her eyes were bright, and the fan blew her white curls off her shoulders.

The years seemed to melt off her face, and for a brief moment I saw the person who was captured in the old brown photo.

The announcer's voice broke my thoughts. *"And she is just flying! Look at her attack that mountain."*

I watched Rachel sail over the last bump with incredible speed, her arms flailing out to the side a bit as she fought to maintain her crouch.

"Pull it together, Rachel. Get control," Mrs. Minton whispered.

And then Rachel was under the banner, and although it seemed like it would be impossible to stop at such a speed, she skidded to a halt in a shower of snow.

The camera cut to the scoreboard. Rachel's time appeared, and the names shifted to show her position.

"Second!" Mrs. Minton yelled. "She's in second! Oh my goodness, what a run!" Mrs. Minton's hand went to her mouth, and her eyes glistened.

"How many are left to race?" Zach asked.

"Quite a few, I'm afraid," she said. "But being in second, even for a while, is quite an accomplishment for a rookie."

I switched on the walkie-talkie. "You can get down for a while, Frank. Rachel's run is over. Over."

"That was the longest 'soon' I have ever known. Over."

"Could you give us a signal every few minutes, Frank? We want to see how Rachel does. She's sitting in second right now. Over."

"Aargh. Over."

Mrs. Minton dabbed her eyes again and leaned back with a sigh.

I let go of the antennae and went to her side. "Is there anything I can get you?"

She shook her head. "How can I ever thank you, Wesley? It meant the world to me to be able to watch Rachel ski."

I felt my face grow red. "Well, let's just say we're even."

The TV crackled, and the picture flickered back. Zach and I ran back to our posts.

"Great run by Marte Tielbaum of Switzerland but not fast enough to catch the leaders. We are still Austria, Canada, France for first, second and third."

The announcers' faces came on the screen.

"Yes, Bob, but let's remember that the strongest skiers are yet to come."

"You're right, Ted, but I have to say, the course is getting slower as the day goes on."

"It looks that way, but can our top three hang on?"

"We'll find out. Here's Austria's golden child. Lotte Meier has won eight of her last ten international races."

"She looked good this morning in training. Let's see how she handles this course."

Beep. Beep. Beeeeeeep.

We watched the screen intently, hoping Frank's arms wouldn't give out until we saw this run.

"She's got such control," Mrs. Minton said "Look how she stays in her tuck." She shook her head in admiration.

"Looks like Lotte is gaining speed on the bottom of this course," the announcer said.

"Yes, Bob. She's an expert at staying low and squeezing every hundredth of a second out of her skis."

Lotte whizzed under the banner and skidded to a stop. Every eye went to the scoreboard.

"And she's done it, Ted! The golden girl has stepped up and taken first place from her teammate. You have to give her credit, that was an amazing run."

"Just two more skiers, Bob. Let's see if they can knock her out of first place."

Zach, Mrs. Minton and I couldn't move. Rachel was third and still in line for a spot on the podium.

I knew Frank must have been in agony, but how could we not watch the next two runs?

The next skier was from Germany, a veteran of World Championship races. When she left the start gate, we held our breath.

Partway down, on a sharp corner, her ski slipped sideways, catching in the icy ruts. That small mistake cost her time. She finished fifth.

One skier to go. I looked at the walkie-talkie. Hang on, Frank, I thought. Just a couple more minutes.

Beep. Beep. Beeeeeep.

The last skier was on course. Her interval times were just off the leader's, and we knew it would be close. As she skied under the banner, everything seemed to morph into slow motion. The camera cut to the scoreboard, and we waited.

A flash of numbers, and the names shifted to show her placing. The last skier had come fourth.

"Oh my goodness!" Mrs. Minton said. "Rachel's got the bronze!"

I lifted my walkie-talkie to let Frank know he could get down just as he walked through the door.

"You found the break?" I asked him.

"It was either that or have permanent tendinitis in my shoulder," he said. "So how'd she do?"

"Third, Frank. She hung on to third." Mrs. Minton's voice quivered. "How can I ever thank you, Frank? And you too, Wesley and Zachariah."

She held out her hand to me. What could I do but walk over to her and take it?

She looked at me very earnestly. "Your father would be so proud of you, Wesley. So proud."

I felt the sting of tears and swallowed hard.

The announcer came on again to let us know the medal ceremony was about to start.

It was an amazing moment when Rachel walked up to the podium wearing her team jacket. An official put the medal around her neck and handed her a bouquet of flowers. Rachel waved to the crowd and then looked straight into the camera. She held up her right hand with her third and fourth fingers bent.

"Oh! The sign!" Mrs. Minton said, her lip trembling with emotion. "That's for me."

"What does it mean?" I asked.

"It's sign language for 'I love you,'" she said and burst into tears.

⸻

A few of weeks after the race, I ran into Mrs. Minton again. She was in Lee's, using a walker to get around.

"Hi, Mrs. Minton," I said, thrilled to see her up and about. "How's the hip?"

"It's coming along, Wesley."

I tried not to let her see me wince at her using my full name in public.

"Oh, I have something for you." She reached into her large shoulder bag and pulled out a ballcap. "Rachel sent this."

It was navy blue with *Pontillo, Chile* embroidered on the front. Under the name was a World Championship pin.

"Wow! This is great," I said. "Thanks."

Mrs. Minton smiled that smile of hers. "Oh, and Wesley…"

"Yes, Mrs. M.?"

"Try to hang on to this one. Okay?"

Acknowledgments

I owe the inspiration for this story to my dad, Fred Rose, whose stories of wild adventures (and misadventures) growing up on Bell Island, Newfoundland, are proof enough of the trouble boys get into.

Heartfelt thanks to all the Kidcritters who helped critique early versions of this story, particularly Hélène Boudreau, Marina Cohen and Marsha Skrypuch.

Special thanks to Richard Bellamy for his valuable information on blasting with dynamite, and to Liam Winters for his great title suggestion.

I would like to thank everyone at Orca, especially my editor, Sarah Harvey, for their hard work, expertise and enthusiasm for this book.

To Craig, Alex, Chelsey, Nathan and Haley: you are part of every book, and your love and support make this all possible.

Natalie Hyde was born in Fredericton, New Brunswick, and grew up in Galt (now Cambridge), Ontario, where she still lives. She spent most of her childhood collecting crickets, toads and tent caterpillars. The rest of the time she practiced being a genie. When that didn't work out, she studied languages at the University of Waterloo. Natalie lives with her husband and four children in a house with too many stairs, which they share with a little leopard gecko and a cat that desperately wants to eat him. *I Owe You One* is Natalie's first book with Orca. To learn more about Natalie, please visit nataliehyde.com.

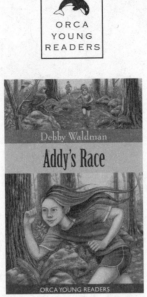

ORCA
YOUNG
READERS

Debby Waldman

Addy's Race

ORCA YOUNG READERS

9781554699247 $7.95 pb

Addy has worn hearing aids for as long as she can remember. Her mother tells her this makes her special, but now that Addy's in grade six, she wants to be special for something she's done. When Addy joins the school running club to keep her best friend, Lucy, company, she discovers she is a gifted runner. Lucy isn't, which is problematic. Further troubles surface when Addy gets paired on a school project with Sierra, a smart, self-assured new classmate who wears a cochlear implant. But is a shared disability enough of a foundation for a friendship? True friends support each other, even if they have different passions and dreams. In the end, Addy discovers she has the power to choose how people will see her, and she does.